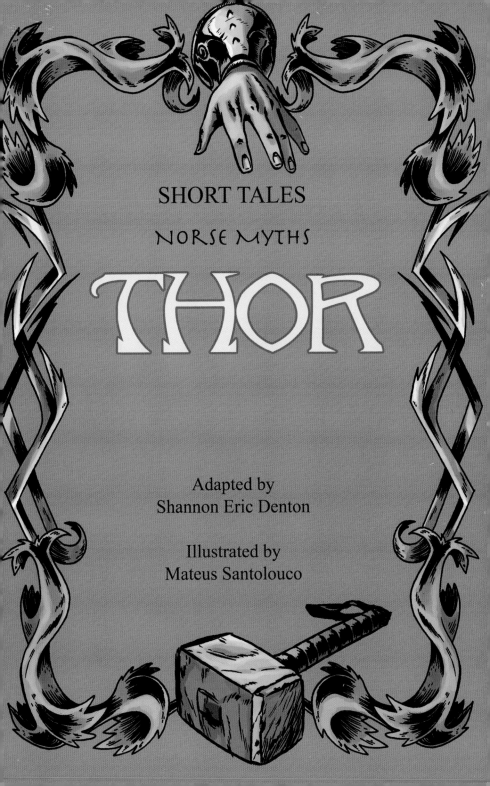

SHORT TALES

NORSE MYTHS

THOR

Adapted by
Shannon Eric Denton

Illustrated by
Mateus Santolouco

visit us at www.abdopublishing.com

Published by Magic Wagon, a division of the ABDO Publishing Group, 8000 West 78th Street, Edina, Minnesota, 55439. Copyright © 2011 by Abdo Consulting Group, Inc. International copyrights reserved in all countries. All rights reserved. No part of this book may be reproduced in any form without written permission from the publisher.

Short Tales ™ is a trademark and logo of Magic Wagon.

Printed in the United States of America, North Mankato, Minnesota.
032010
092010
This book contains at least 10% recycled materials.

Adapted Text by Shannon Eric Denton
Illustrations by Mateus Santolouco
Colors by Milen Parvanov
Edited by Stephanie Hedlund and Rochelle Baltzer
Interior Layout by Kristen Fitzner Denton
Book Design and Packaging by Shannon Eric Denton

Library of Congress Cataloging-in-Publication Data

Denton, Shannon Eric.
  Thor / adapted by Shannon Eric Denton ; illustrated by Mateus Santolouco.
    p. cm. -- (Short tales. Norse myths)
  ISBN 978-1-60270-569-2
  1. Thor (Norse deity)--Juvenile literature. I. Santolouco, Mateus, 1979- II. Title.
  BL870.T5D46 2009
  398.209363'01--dc22
                    2008032495

THE NORSE GODS

ODIN:
The All-Father
of the Gods

FRIGGA:
Queen of
the Gods

BALDUR:
The Best Loved
of the Gods

FORSETI:
God of
Justice

HEIMDALL:
The Guardian
of Asgard

HOD:
God of Winter

THOR:
God of Thunder

TYR:
God of War

HERMOD:
Messenger of
the Gods

FREYR:
God of Weather

LOKI:
The Trickster

FREYA:
Goddess of
Beauty and Love

Mythical Beginnings

In ancient Asgard a redheaded boy was born to Odin and Frigga, the king and queen of the gods. Odin named this boy Thor. . .

Thor had two older brothers named Baldur and Hoor. Hoor was blind, but that didn't stop the three brothers from having fun together. Thor, Baldur, and Hoor got into lots of trouble.

When Thor was a teenager, Odin left on a quest to find a cure for Hoor's blindness. Without their father, the brothers got into even more trouble.

Thor was the youngest. But, he soon grew to be the biggest of the three brothers. His strength impressed everyone. Thor liked to show off, especially for a young woman named Sif.

Thor wanted to marry Sif. But before he could, war broke out between two groups of gods. The war was fierce, and all of Asgard fought in it.

The war lasted for many years. Thor proved himself to be the mightiest of all Asgard's warriors.

Thor fought with a magical hammer called Mjolnir. Every time Thor threw Mjolnir at his enemies, it returned to him.

Mjolnir also had the power to create lightning bolts. Thor needed extra strength to lift mighty Mjolnir. So, he wore the magical belt Megingjord.

After many years of fighting, the war was finally over. Neither side had won. Instead, the two groups became one society, never to fight again.

The warriors celebrated the newfound peace in Asgard. They danced and feasted.

During the feast, Thor asked Sif to marry him. She agreed.

Soon after, Thor married Sif. It was a beautiful spring day. His whole family celebrated with them.

Thor and Sif had three children. They named their sons Magni and Modi. They named their daughter Thrud.

Thor and Sif were very happy. But, Thor missed his adventures in battle. He also missed his father, Odin.

Thor decided to find his father. So, Thor, Hoor, and Baldur set out in search of Odin.

Thor, Hoor, and Baldur rode to the edge of Asgard and beyond. They even entered Jotunheim, the land of the giants.

Many frost giants attacked the brothers as they searched for their father. But after years of war, the three brothers had become very good at fighting.

Thor defeated many of the frost giants. One giant pleaded for his life after losing a fight. He offered Thor a special gift from within his barn.

Thor thought the giant was trying to trick them. But, he followed the giant into his barn anyway.

The giant did indeed trick Thor, but not how Thor thought he would. Thor left the barn with a pair of giant goats.

Thor was able to control the goats. He drove them attached to a chariot. Soon, the brothers continued their quest to find their father.

Thor, Baldur, and Hoor searched all of Earth. But, Odin could not be found. So, the brothers decided to return to Asgard.

The brothers returned home to find a stranger named Loki had come to Asgard. Loki was popular, but he grew jealous of the love Asgard's people showed the brothers. Loki began to plot against them.

Loki tricked a man into killing Baldur. The gods drove Loki out, and all of Asgard wept for Baldur.

Many years later, Loki and his army of giants waged war on the gods. The battle was called Ragnarok.

Thor defeated the monstrous Midgard serpent. But, he was killed by its poison. Before he died, Thor passed mighty Mjolnir on to his children.

As the flames of Ragnarok died out, a beautiful new world was born. The old gods were gone forever. But, the Norse people would always remember the heroic Thor. They honored him by naming Thursday after him!